A·A·MILNE

WINNIE-THE-POOH

A TREASURY OF
STORIES, HUMS AND VERSE

WITH ILLUSTRATIONS BY E·H·SHEPARD

METHUEN

First Published in 1993
Reprinted 1995
Produced in 1995 exclusively for W. H. Smith Limited
Greenbridge Road, Swindon, Wiltshire SN3 3LD
by Methuen Children's Books
a division of Reed Children's Books
Michelin House, 81 Fulham Road, London SW3 6RB
and Auckland, Melbourne, Singapore and Toronto
Copyright © 1993 by Michael John Brown, Peter Janson-Smith,
Roger Hugh Vaughan Charles Morgan and Timothy Michael Robinson
Trustees of the Pooh Properties

Text by A. A. Milne and line illustrations by Ernest. H. Shepard
from *Winnie-the-Pooh* and *The House at Pooh Corner*
copyright under the Berne Convention.
Colouring of the illustrations copyright © 1970
by Ernest H. Shepard and Methuen and Co. Ltd.
and copyright © 1973,1974 by Ernest H. Shepard and Methuen Children's Books Ltd.

Text by A. A. Milne and line illustrations by E. H. Shepard from
When We Were Very Young and *Now We Are Six*
copyright under the Berne Convention
Colouring of the illustrations by Mark Burgess
copyright © 1989 by Methuen Children's Books
Cover design by Brian Voakes

Printed and bound by Graficromo s.a., Cordoba, Spain

ISBN 0 416 18845 1

British Library and Catalogue-in-Publishing Data
A Catalogue record for this book is available from the British Library

Contents

Winnie-the-Pooh and Some Bees

Here is Edward Bear, coming downstairs now, bump, bump, bump, on the back of his head, behind Christopher Robin. It is, as far as he knows, the only way of coming downstairs, but sometimes he feels that there really is another way, if only he could stop bumping for a moment and think of it. And then he feels that perhaps there isn't. Anyhow, here he is at the bottom, and ready to be introduced to you. Winnie-the-Pooh.

When I first heard his name, I said, just as you are going to say, 'But I thought he was a boy?'

'So did I,' said Christopher Robin.

'Then you can't call him Winnie?'

'I don't.'

'But you said —'

'He's Winnie-ther-Pooh. Don't you know what "*ther*" means?'

'Ah, yes, now I do,' I said quickly; and I hope you do too, because it is all the explanation you are going to get.

Sometimes Winnie-the-Pooh likes a game of some sort when he comes downstairs, and sometimes he likes to sit quietly in front of the fire and listen to a story. This evening —

'What about a story?' said Christopher Robin.

'*What* about a story?' I said.

'Could you very sweetly tell Winnie-the-Pooh one?'

'I suppose I could,' I said. 'What sort of stories does he like?'

'About himself. Because he's *that* sort of Bear.'

'Oh, I see.'

'So could you very sweetly?'

'I'll try,' I said.

So I tried.

Once upon a time, a very long time ago now, about last Friday, Winnie-the-Pooh lived in a forest all by himself under the name of Sanders.

('What does "under the name" mean?' asked Christopher Robin.

'It means he had the name over the door in gold letters and lived under it.'

'Winnie-the-Pooh wasn't quite sure,' said Christopher Robin.

'Now I am,' said a growly voice.

'Then I will go on,' said I.)

One day when he was out walking, he came to an open place in the middle of the forest, and in the middle of this place was a large oak-tree, and, from the top of the tree, there came a loud buzzing-noise.

Winnie-the-Pooh sat down at the foot of the tree, put his head between his paws, and began to think.

First of all he said to himself: 'That buzzing-noise means something. You don't get a buzzing-noise like that, just buzzing and buzzing, without its meaning something. If there's a buzzing-noise, somebody's making a buzzing-noise, and the only reason for making a buzzing-noise that *I* know of is because you're a bee.'

Then he thought another long time, and said: 'And the only reason for being a bee that I know of is making honey.'

And then he got up, and said: 'And the only reason for making honey is so as *I* can eat it.'

So he began to climb the tree.

He
climbed
and
he
climbed
and
he
climbed,
and
as
he
climbed
he sang
a
little
song
to
himself.
It
went
like
this:

Isn't it funny
How a bear likes honey?
Buzz! Buzz! Buzz!
I wonder why he does?

Then he climbed a little further . . . and a little further . . . and then just a little further. By that time he had thought of another song.

It's a very funny thought that, if Bears were Bees,
They'd build their nests at the *bottom* of trees.
And that being so (if the Bees were Bears),
We shouldn't have to climb up all these stairs.

He was getting rather tired by this time, so that is why he sang a Complaining Song. He was nearly there now, and if he just stood on that branch . . . *Crack!*

'Oh, help!' said Pooh, as he dropped ten feet on to the branch below him.

'If only I hadn't —' he said, as he bounced twenty feet on to the next branch.

'You see, what I *meant* to do,' he explained, as he turned head-over-heels, and crashed on to another branch thirty feet below, 'what I *meant* to do —'

'Of course, it *was* rather —' he admitted, as he slithered very quickly through the next six branches.

'It all comes, I suppose,' he decided, as he said good-bye to the last branch, spun round three times, and flew gracefully into a gorse-bush, 'it all comes of *liking* honey so much. Oh, help!'

He crawled out of the gorse-bush, brushed the prickles from his nose, and began to think again. And the first person he thought of was Christopher Robin.

(*'Was that me?' said Christopher Robin in an awed voice, hardly daring to believe it.*

'That was you.'

14

Christopher Robin said nothing, but his eyes got larger and larger, and his face got pinker and pinker.)

So Winnie-the-Pooh went round to his friend Christopher Robin, who lived behind a green door in another part of the Forest.

'Good morning, Christopher Robin,' he said.

'Good morning, Winnie-*ther*-Pooh,' said you.

'I wonder if you've got such a thing as a balloon about you?'

'A balloon?'

'Yes, I just said to myself coming along: "I wonder if Christopher Robin has such a thing as a balloon about him?" I just said it to myself, thinking of balloons, and wondering.'

'What do you want a balloon for?' you said.

Winnie-the-Pooh looked round to see that nobody was listening, put his paw to his mouth, and said in a deep whisper: *'Honey!'*

'But you don't get honey with balloons!'

'*I* do,' said Pooh.

Well, it just happened that you had been to a party the day before at the house of your friend Piglet, and you had balloons at the party. You had had a big green balloon; and one of Rabbit's relations had had a big blue one, and had left it behind, being really too young to go to a party at all; and so you had brought the green one *and* the blue one home with you.

'Which one would you like?' you asked Pooh.

He put his head between his paws and thought very carefully.

'It's like this,' he said. 'When you go after honey with a balloon, the great thing is not to let the bees know you're coming. Now, if you have a green balloon, they might think you were only part of the tree, and not notice you, and if you have a blue balloon, they might think you were only part of the sky, and not notice you, and the question is: Which is most likely?'

'Wouldn't they notice *you* underneath the balloon?' you asked.

'They might or they might not,' said Winnie-the-Pooh. 'You never can tell with bees.' He thought for a moment and said: 'I shall try to look like a small black cloud. That will deceive them.'

'Then you had better have the blue balloon,' you said; and so it was decided.

Well, you both went out with the blue balloon, and you took your gun with you, just in case, as you always did, and Winnie-the-Pooh went to a very muddy place that he knew of, and rolled and rolled until he was black all over; and then, when the balloon was blown up

as big as big, and you and Pooh were both holding on to the string, you let go suddenly, and Pooh Bear floated gracefully up into the sky, and stayed there – level with the top of the tree and about twenty feet away from it.

'Hooray!' you shouted.

'Isn't that fine?' shouted Winnie-the-Pooh down to you. 'What do I look like?'

19

'You look like a Bear holding on to a balloon,' you said.

'Not,' said Pooh anxiously, '– not like a small black cloud in a blue sky?'

'Not very much.'

'Ah, well, perhaps from up here it looks different. And, as I say, you never can tell with bees.'

There was no wind to blow him nearer to the tree so there he stayed. He could see the honey, he could smell the honey, but he couldn't quite reach the honey.

After a little while he called down to you.

'Christopher Robin!' he said in a loud whisper.

'Hallo!'

'I think the bees *suspect* something!'

'What sort of thing?'

'I don't know. But something tells me that they're *suspicious*!'

'Perhaps they think that you're after their honey?'

'It may be that. You never can tell with bees.'

There was another little silence, and then he called down to you again.

'Christopher Robin!'

'Yes?'

'Have you an umbrella in your house?'

'I think so.'

'I wish you would bring it out here, and walk up and down with it, and look up at me every now and then, and say "Tut-tut, it looks like rain." I think, if you did that, it would help the deception which we are practising on these bees.'

Well, you laughed to yourself, 'Silly old Bear!' but you didn't say it aloud because you were so fond of him, and you went home for your umbrella.

'Oh, there you are!' called down Winnie-the-Pooh, as soon as you got back to the tree. 'I was beginning to get anxious. I have discovered that the bees are now definitely Suspicious.'

'Shall I put my umbrella up?' you said.

'Yes, but wait a moment. We must be practical. The important bee to deceive is the Queen Bee. Can you see which is the Queen Bee from down there?'

'No.'

'A pity. Well, now, if you walk up and down with your umbrella, saying, "Tut-tut, it looks like rain," I shall do what I can by singing a little Cloud Song, such as a cloud might sing. . . . Go!'

So, while you walked up and down and wondered if it would rain, Winnie-the-Pooh sang this song:

How sweet to be a Cloud
    Floating in the Blue!
Every little cloud
Always sings aloud.

'How sweet to be a Cloud
    Floating in the Blue!'
It makes him very proud
To be a little cloud.

The bees were still buzzing as suspiciously as ever. Some of them, indeed, left their nests and flew all round the cloud as it began the second verse of this song, and one bee sat down on the nose of the cloud for a moment, and then got up again.

'Christopher – *ow!* – Robin,' called out the cloud.

'Yes?'

'I have just been thinking, and I have come to a very important decision. *These are the wrong sort of bees.*'

'Are they?'

'Quite the wrong sort. So I should think they would make the wrong sort of honey, shouldn't you?'

'Would they?'

'Yes. So I think I shall come down.'

'How?' asked you.

Winnie-the-Pooh hadn't thought about this. If he let go of the string, he would fall – *bump* – and he didn't like the idea of that. So he thought for a long time, and then he said:

'Christopher Robin, you must shoot the balloon with your gun. Have you got your gun?'

'Of course I have,' you said. 'But if I do that, it will spoil the balloon,' you said.

'But if you *don't*,' said Pooh, 'I shall have to let go, and that would spoil *me*.'

When he put it like this, you saw how it was, and you aimed very carefully at the balloon, and fired.

'*Ow!*' said Pooh.

'Did I miss?' you asked.

'You didn't exactly *miss*,' said Pooh, 'but you missed the *balloon*.'

'I'm so sorry,' you said, and you fired again, and this time you hit the balloon, and the air came slowly out, and Winnie-the-Pooh floated down to the ground.

But his arms were so stiff from holding on to the string of the balloon all that time that they stayed up straight in the air for more than a week, and whenever a fly came and settled on his nose he had to blow it off. And I think – but I am not sure – that *that* is why he was always called Pooh.

'Is that the end of the story?' asked Christopher Robin.

'That's the end of that one. There are others.'

'About Pooh and Me?'

'And Piglet and Rabbit and all of you. Don't you remember?'

'I do remember, and then when I try to remember, I forget.'

'That day when Pooh and Piglet tried to catch the Heffalump —'

'They didn't catch it, did they?'

'No.'

'Pooh couldn't, because he hasn't any brain. Did *I* catch it?'

'Well, that comes into the story.'

Christopher Robin nodded.

'I do remember,' he said, 'only Pooh doesn't very well, so that's why he likes having it told to him again. Because then it's a real story and not just a remembering.'

'That's just how *I* feel,' I said.

Christopher Robin gave a deep sigh, picked his Bear up by the leg, and walked off to the door, trailing Pooh behind him. At the door he turned and said, 'Coming to see me have my bath?'

'I might,' I said.

'I didn't hurt him when I shot him, did I?'

'Not a bit.'

He nodded and went out, and in a moment I heard Winnie-the-Pooh – *bump, bump, bump* – going up the stairs behind him.

Teddy Bear

A bear, however hard he tries,
Grows tubby without exercise.
Our Teddy Bear is short and fat,
Which is not to be wondered at;
He gets what exercise he can
By falling off the ottoman,
But generally seems to lack
The energy to clamber back.

Now tubbiness is just the thing
Which gets a fellow wondering;
And teddy worried lots about
The fact that he was rather stout.
He thought: 'If only I were thin!
But how does anyone begin?'
He thought: 'It really isn't fair
To grudge me exercise and air.'

26

A bear, however hard he tries,
Grows tubby without exercise.
Our Teddy Bear is short and fat,
Which is not to be wondered at.
But do you think it worries him
To know that he is far from slim?
No, just the other way about —
He's *proud* of being short and stout.

For Stoutness Exercises

Tra-la-la, tra-la-la,
Tra-la-la, tra-la-la.
Rum-tum-tiddle-um-tum.
Tiddle-iddle, tiddle-iddle,
Tiddle-iddle, tiddle-iddle,
Rum-tum-tum-tiddle-um.

Piglet is Entirely Surrounded by Water

It rained and it rained and it rained. Piglet told himself that never in all his life, and *he* was goodness knows *how* old – three, was it, or four? – never had he seen so much rain. Days and days and days.

'If only,' he thought, as he looked out of the window, 'I had been in Pooh's house, or Christopher Robin's house, or Rabbit's house when it began to rain, then I should have had Company all this time, instead of being here all alone, with nothing to do except wonder when it will stop.' And he imagined himself with Pooh, saying, 'Did you ever see such rain, Pooh?' and Pooh saying, 'Isn't it *awful*, Piglet?' and Piglet saying, 'I wonder how it is over Christopher Robin's way,' and Pooh saying, 'I should think poor old Rabbit is about flooded out by this time.' It would have been jolly to talk like this, and really, it wasn't much good having anything exciting like floods, if you couldn't share them with somebody.

For it was rather exciting. The little dry ditches in which Piglet had nosed about so often had become streams, the little streams across which he had splashed were rivers, and the river, between whose steep banks they had played so happily, had sprawled out of its own bed and was taking up so much room everywhere, that Piglet was beginning to wonder whether it would be coming into *his* bed soon.

'It's a little Anxious,' he said to himself, 'to be a Very Small Animal Entirely Surrounded by Water. Christopher Robin and Pooh could escape by Climbing Trees, and Kanga could escape by Jumping, and Rabbit could escape by Burrowing, and Owl could escape by Flying, and Eeyore could escape by – by Making a Loud Noise Until Rescued, and here am I, surrounded by water and I can't do *anything*.'

It went on raining, and every day the water got a little higher, until now it was nearly up to Piglet's window . . . and still he hadn't done anything.

'There's Pooh,' he thought to himself. 'Pooh hasn't much Brain, but he never comes to any harm. He does silly things and they turn out right. There's Owl. Owl hasn't exactly got Brain, but he Knows Things. He would know the Right Thing to Do when Surrounded by Water. There's Rabbit. He hasn't Learnt in Books, but he can always Think of a Clever Plan. There's Kanga. She isn't Clever, Kanga isn't, but she would be so anxious about Roo that she would do a Good Thing to Do without thinking about it. And then there's Eeyore. And Eeyore is so miserable anyhow that he wouldn't mind about this. But I wonder what Christopher Robin would do?'

Then suddenly he remembered a story which Christopher Robin had told him about a man on a desert island who had written something in a bottle and thrown it into the sea; and Piglet thought that if he wrote something in a bottle and threw it in the water, perhaps somebody would come and rescue *him!*

He left the window and began to search his house, all of it that wasn't under water, and at last he found a pencil and a small piece of dry paper, and a bottle with a cork to it. And he wrote on one side of the paper:

HELP!
PIGLIT (ME)

and on the other side:

IT'S ME PIGLIT, HELP HELP!

Then he put the paper in the bottle, and he corked the bottle up as tightly as he could, and leant out of his window as far as he could lean without falling in, and he threw the bottle as far as he could

throw – *splash!* – and in a little while it bobbed up again on the water; and he watched it floating slowly away in the distance, until his eyes ached with looking, and sometimes he thought it was the bottle, and sometimes he thought it was just a ripple on the water which he was following, and then suddenly he knew that he would never see it again and that he had done all that he could do to save himself.

'So now,' he thought, 'somebody else will have to do something, and I hope they will do it soon, because if they don't I shall have to swim, which I can't, so I hope they do it soon.' And then he gave a very long sigh and said, 'I wish Pooh were here. It's so much more friendly with two.'

When the rain began Pooh was asleep. It rained, and it rained, and it rained, and he slept and he slept and he slept. He had had a tiring day. You remember how he discovered the North Pole; well, he was so proud of this that he asked Christopher Robin if there were any other Poles such as a Bear of Little Brain might discover.

'There's a South Pole,' said Christopher Robin, 'and I expect there's an East Pole and a West Pole, though people don't like talking about them.'

Pooh was very excited when he heard this, and suggested that they should have an Expotition to discover the East Pole, but Christopher Robin had thought of something else to do with Kanga; so Pooh went out to discover the East Pole by himself. Whether he discovered it or not, I forget; but he was so tired when he got home that, in the very middle of his supper, after he had been eating for little more than half-an-hour, he fell fast asleep in his chair, and slept and slept and slept.

Then suddenly he was dreaming. He was at the East Pole, and it was a very cold pole with the coldest sort of snow and ice all over it. He had found a beehive to sleep in, but there wasn't room for his legs, so he had left them outside. And Wild Woozles, such as inhabit the East Pole, came and nibbled all the fur off his legs to make Nests for their Young. And the more they nibbled, the colder his legs got, until suddenly he woke up with an *Ow!* – and there he was, sitting in his chair with his feet in the water, and water all round him!

He splashed to his door and looked out. . . .

'This is Serious,' said Pooh. 'I must have an Escape.'

So he took his largest pot of honey and escaped with it to a broad branch of his tree, well above the water, and then he climbed down again and escaped with another pot . . . and when the whole Escape was finished, there was Pooh sitting on his branch, dangling his legs, and there, beside him, were ten pots of honey. . . .

Two days later, there was Pooh, sitting on his branch, dangling his legs, and there, beside him, were four pots of honey. . . .

Three days later, there was Pooh, sitting on his branch, dangling his legs, and there beside him, was one pot of honey.

Four days later, there was Pooh . . .

And it was on the morning of the fourth day that Piglet's bottle came floating past him, and with one loud cry of 'Honey!' Pooh plunged into the water, seized the bottle, and struggled back to his tree again.

'Bother!' said Pooh, as he opened it. 'All that wet for nothing. What's that bit of paper doing?'

He took it out and looked at it.

'It's a Missage,' he said to himself, 'that's what it is. And that letter is a "P," and so is that, and so is that, and "P" means "Pooh," so it's a very important Missage to me, and I can't read it. I must find Christopher Robin or Owl or Piglet, one of those Clever Readers who can read things, and they will tell me what this message means. Only I can't swim. Bother!'

Then he had an idea, and I think that for a Bear of Very Little Brain, it was a good idea. He said to himself:

'If a bottle can float, then a jar can float, and if a jar floats, I can sit on the top of it, if it's a very big jar.'

So he took his biggest jar, and corked it up.

'All boats have to have a name,' he said, 'so I shall call mine *The Floating Bear*.'

And with these words he dropped his boat into the water and jumped in after it.

For a little while Pooh and *The Floating Bear* were uncertain as to which of them was meant to be on the top, but after trying one or two different positions, they settled down with *The Floating Bear* underneath and Pooh triumphantly astride it, paddling vigorously with his feet.

Christopher Robin lived at the very top of the Forest. It rained, and it rained, and it rained, but the water couldn't come up to *his* house. It was rather jolly to look down into the valleys and see the water all round him, but it rained so hard that he stayed indoors most of the time, and thought about things. Every morning he went out with his umbrella and put a stick in the place where the water came up to, and every next morning he went out and couldn't see his stick any more, so he put another stick in the place where the water came up to, and then he walked home again, and each morning he had a shorter way to walk than he had had the morning before. On the morning of the fifth day he saw the water all round him, and knew that for the first time in his life he was on a real island. Which was very exciting.

It was on this morning that Owl came flying over the water to say 'How do you do?' to his friend Christopher Robin.

'I say, Owl,' said Christopher Robin, 'isn't this fun? I'm on an island!'

'The atmospheric conditions have been very unfavourable lately,' said Owl.

'The what?'

'It has been raining,' explained Owl.

'Yes,' said Christopher Robin. 'It has.'

'The flood-level has reached an unprecedented height.'

'The who?'

'There's a lot of water about,' explained Owl.

'Yes,' said Christopher Robin, 'there is.'

'However, the prospects are rapidly becoming more favourable. At any moment —'

'Have you seen Pooh?'

'No. At any moment —'

'I hope he's all right,' said Christopher Robin. 'I've been wondering about him. I expect Piglet's with him. Do you think they're all right, Owl?'

'I expect so. You see, at any moment —'

'Do go and see, Owl. Because Pooh hasn't got very much brain, and he might do something silly, and I do love him so, Owl. Do you see, Owl?'

'That's all right,' said Owl, 'I'll go. Back directly.' And he flew off.
In a little while he was back again.

'Pooh isn't there,' he said.

'Not there?'

'He's *been* there. He's been
sitting on a branch of his tree
outside his house with nine pots
of honey. But he isn't there now.'

'Oh, Pooh!' cried Christopher
Robin. 'Where *are* you?'

'Here I am,' said a growly
voice behind him.

'Pooh!'

They rushed into each other's arms.

'How did you get here, Pooh?' asked Christopher Robin, when he
was ready to talk again.

'On my boat,' said Pooh proudly. 'I had a Very Important Missage
sent me in a bottle, and owing to having got some water in my eyes, I
couldn't read it, so I brought it to you. On my boat.'

With these proud words he gave Christopher Robin the missage.

'But it's from Piglet!' cried Christopher Robin when he had read it.

'Isn't there anything about Pooh in it?' asked Bear, looking over
his shoulder.

Christopher Robin read the message aloud.

'Oh, are those "P's" piglets? I thought they were poohs.'

'We must rescue him at once! I thought he was with *you*, Pooh.
Owl, could you rescue him on your back?'

'I don't think so,' said Owl, after grave thought. 'It is doubtful if
the necessary dorsal muscles —'

'Then would you fly to him at *once* and say that Rescue is Coming?

And Pooh and I will think of a Rescue and come as quick as ever we can. Oh, don't *talk*, Owl, go on quick!' And, still thinking of something to say, Owl flew off.

'Now then, Pooh,' said Christopher Robin, 'where's your boat?'

'I ought to say,' explained Pooh as they walked down to the shore of the island, 'that it isn't just an ordinary sort of boat. Sometimes it's a Boat, and sometimes it's more of an Accident. It all depends.'

'Depends on what?'

'On whether I'm on the top of it or underneath it.'

'Oh! Well, where is it?'

'There!' said Pooh, pointing proudly to *The Floating Bear*.

It wasn't what Christopher Robin

expected, and the more he looked at it, the more he thought what a Brave and Clever Bear Pooh was, and the more Christopher Robin thought this, the more Pooh looked modestly down his nose and tried to pretend he wasn't.

'But it's too small for two of us,' said Christopher Robin sadly.

'Three of us with Piglet.'

'That makes it smaller still. Oh, Pooh Bear, what shall we do?'

And then this Bear, Pooh Bear, Winnie-the-Pooh, F.O.P. (Friend of Piglet's), R.C. (Rabbit's Companion), P.D. (Pole Discoverer), E.C. and T.F. (Eeyore's Comforter and Tail-finder) – in fact, Pooh himself – said something so clever that Christopher Robin could only look at him with mouth open and eyes staring, wondering if this was really the Bear of Very Little Brain whom he had known and loved so long.

'We might go in your umbrella,'
said Pooh.
'?'
'We might go in your umbrella,'
said Pooh.
'? ?'
'We might go in your umbrella,'
said Pooh.
'!!!!!'

For suddenly Christopher Robin saw that they might. He opened his umbrella and put it point downwards in the water. It floated but wobbled. Pooh got in. He was just beginning to say that it was all right now, when he found that it wasn't, so after a short drink, which he didn't really want, he waded back to Christopher Robin. Then they both got in together, and it wobbled no longer.

'I shall call this boat *The Brain of Pooh*,' said Christopher Robin, and *The Brain of Pooh* set sail forthwith in a south-westerly direction, revolving gracefully.

You can imagine Piglet's joy when at last the ship came in sight of him. In after-years he liked to think that he had been in Very Great Danger during the Terrible Flood, but the only danger he had really been in was the last half-hour of his imprisonment, when Owl, who

had just flown up, sat on a branch of his tree to comfort him, and told him a very long story about an aunt who had once laid a seagull's egg by mistake, and the story went on and on, rather like this sentence, until Piglet who was listening out of his window without much hope, went to sleep quietly and naturally, slipping slowly out of the window towards the water until he was only hanging on by his toes, at which moment, luckily, a sudden loud squawk from Owl, which was really part of the story, being what his aunt said, woke the Piglet up and just gave him time to jerk himself back into safety and say, 'How interesting, and did she?' when — well, you can imagine his joy when at last he saw the good ship, *Brain of Pooh* (*Captain*, C. Robin; *1st Mate*, P. Bear) coming over the sea to rescue him. . . .

And as that is really the end of the story, and I am very tired after that last sentence, I think I shall stop there.

Furry Bear

If I were a bear,
   And a big bear too,
I shouldn't much care
   If it froze or snew;
I shouldn't much mind
   If it snowed or friz —
I'd be all fur-lined
   With a coat like his!

For I'd have fur boots and a brown fur wrap,
And brown fur knickers and a big fur cap.
I'd have a fur muffle-ruff to cover my jaws,
And brown fur mittens on my big brown paws.
With a big brown furry-down up to my head,
I'd sleep all the winter in a big fur bed.

Sing Ho! For the Life of a Bear

Sing Ho! for the life of a Bear!
Sing Ho! for the life of a Bear!
I don't much mind if it rains or snows,
'Cos I've got a lot of honey on my nice new nose!
I don't much care if it snows or thaws,
'Cos I've got a lot of honey on my nice clean paws!
Sing Ho! for a Bear!
Sing Ho! for a Pooh!
And I'll have a little something in an hour or two!

The Friend

There are lots and lots of people who are always asking things,
Like Dates and Pounds-and-ounces and the names of funny Kings,
And the answer's either Sixpence or A Hundred Inches Long.
And I know they'll think me silly if I get the answer wrong.

So Pooh and I go whispering, and Pooh looks very bright,
And says, 'Well, *I* say sixpence, but I don't suppose I'm right.'
And then it doesn't matter what the answer ought to be,
'Cos if he's right, I'm Right, and if he's wrong, it isn't Me.

Eeyore has a Birthday

Eeyore, the old grey Donkey, stood by the side of the stream, and looked at himself in the water.

'Pathetic,' he said. 'That's what it is. Pathetic.'

He turned and walked slowly down the stream for twenty yards, splashed across it, and walked slowly back on the other side. Then he looked at himself in the water again.

'As I thought,' he said. 'No better from *this* side. But nobody minds. Nobody cares. Pathetic, that's what it is.'

There was a crackling noise in the bracken behind him, and out came Pooh.

'Good morning, Eeyore,' said Pooh.

'Good morning, Pooh Bear,' said Eeyore gloomily. 'If it *is* a good morning,' he said. 'Which I doubt,' said he.

'Why, what's the matter?'

'Nothing, Pooh Bear, nothing. We can't all, and some of us don't. That's all there is to it.'

'Can't all *what*?' said Pooh, rubbing his nose.

'Gaiety. Song-and-dance. Here we go round the mulberry bush.'

'Oh!' said Pooh. He thought for a long time, and then asked, 'What mulberry bush is that?'

'Bon-hommy,' went on Eeyore gloomily. 'French word meaning bonhommy,' he explained. 'I'm not complaining, but There It Is.'

Pooh sat down on a large stone, and tried to think this out. It sounded to him like a riddle, and he was never much good at riddles, being a Bear of Very Little Brain. So he sang *Cottleston Pie* instead:

> Cottleston, Cottleston, Cottleston Pie.
> A fly can't bird, but a bird can fly.
> Ask me a riddle and I reply:
> *'Cottleston, Cottleston, Cottleston Pie.'*

That was the first verse. When he had finished it, Eeyore didn't actually say that he didn't like it, so Pooh very kindly sang the second verse to him:

Cottleston, Cottleston, Cottleston Pie,
A fish can't whistle and neither can I.
Ask me a riddle and I reply:
'Cottleston, Cottleston, Cottleston Pie.'

Eeyore still said nothing at all, so Pooh hummed the third verse quietly to himself:

Cottleston, Cottleston, Cottleston Pie,
Why does a chicken, I don't know why.
Ask me a riddle and I reply:
'Cottleston, Cottleston, Cottleston Pie.'

'That's right,' said Eeyore. 'Sing. Umpty-tiddly, umpty-too. Here we go gathering Nuts and May. Enjoy yourself.'

'I am,' said Pooh.

'Some can,' said Eeyore.

'Why, what's the matter?'

'*Is* anything the matter?'

'You seem so sad, Eeyore.'

'Sad? Why should I be sad? It's my birthday. The happiest day of the year.'

'Your birthday?' said Pooh in great surprise.

'Of course it is. Can't you see? Look at all the presents I have had.' He waved a foot from side to side. 'Look at the birthday cake. Candles and pink sugar.'

Pooh looked – first to the right and then to the left.

'Presents?' said Pooh. 'Birthday cake?' said Pooh. '*Where?*'

'Can't you see them?'

'No,' said Pooh.

'Neither can I,' said Eeyore. 'Joke,' he explained. 'Ha ha!'

Pooh scratched his head, being a little puzzled by all this.

'But is it really your birthday?' he asked.

'It is.'

'Oh! Well, many happy returns of the day, Eeyore.'

'And many happy returns to you, Pooh Bear.'

'But it isn't *my* birthday.'

'No, it's mine.'

'But you said "Many happy returns" —'

'Well, why not? You don't always want to be miserable on my birthday, do you?'

'Oh, I see,' said Pooh.

'It's bad enough,' said Eeyore, almost breaking down, 'being miserable myself, what with no presents and no cake and no candles, and no proper notice taken of me at all, but if everybody else is going to be miserable too —'

This was too much for Pooh. 'Stay there!' he called to Eeyore, as he turned and hurried back home as quick as he could; for he felt that he must get poor Eeyore a present of *some* sort at once, and he could always think of a proper one afterwards.

Outside his house he found Piglet, jumping up and down trying to reach the knocker.

'Hallo, Piglet,' he said.

'Hallo, Pooh,' said Piglet.

'What are *you* trying to do?'

'I was trying to reach the knocker,' said Piglet.
'I just came round —'

'Let me do it for you,' said Pooh kindly. So he reached up and knocked at the door. 'I have just seen Eeyore,' he began, 'and poor Eeyore is in a Very Sad Condition, because it's his birthday, and nobody has taken any notice of it, and he's very Gloomy – you know what Eeyore is – and there he was, and – What a long time whoever lives here is answering this door.' And he knocked again.

'But, Pooh,' said Piglet, 'it's your own house!'

'Oh!' said Pooh. 'So it is,' he said. 'Well, let's go in.'

So in they went. The first thing Pooh did was to go to the cupboard to see if he had quite a small jar of honey left; and he had, so he took it down.

'I'm giving this to Eeyore,' he explained, 'as a present. What are *you* going to give?'

'Couldn't I give it too?' said Piglet. 'From both of us?'

'No,' said Pooh. 'That would *not* be a good plan.'

'All right, then, I'll give him a balloon. I've got one left from my party. I'll go and get it now, shall I?'

'That, Piglet, is a *very* good idea. It is just what Eeyore wants to cheer him up. Nobody can be uncheered with a balloon.'

So off Piglet trotted; and in the other direction went Pooh, with his jar of honey.

It was a warm day, and he had a long way to go. He hadn't gone more than half-way when a sort of funny feeling began to creep all over him. It began at the tip of his nose and trickled all through him and out at the soles of his feet. It was just as if somebody inside him were saying, 'Now then, Pooh, time for a little something.'

'Dear, dear,' said Pooh, 'I didn't know it was as late as that.' So he sat down and took the top off his jar of honey. 'Lucky I brought this with me,' he thought. 'Many a bear going out on a warm day like this would never have thought of bringing a little something with him.'

And he began to eat.

'Now let me see,' he thought, as he took his last lick of the inside of the jar, 'where was I going? Ah, yes, Eeyore.' He got up slowly.

And then, suddenly, he remembered. He had eaten Eeyore's birthday present!

'*Bother!*' said Pooh. 'What *shall* I do? I *must* give him *something*.'

For a little while he couldn't think of anything. Then he thought: 'Well, it's a very nice pot, even if there's no honey in it, and if I washed it clean, and got somebody to write '*A Happy Birthday*' on it, Eeyore could keep things in it, which might be Useful.' So, as he was just passing the Hundred Acre Wood, he went inside to call on Owl, who lived there.

'Good morning, Owl,' he said.

'Good morning, Pooh,' said Owl.

'Many happy returns of Eeyore's birthday,' said Pooh.

'Oh, is that what it is?'

'What are you giving him, Owl?'

'What are *you* giving him, Pooh?'

'I'm giving him a Useful Pot to Keep Things In, and I wanted to ask you —'

'Is this it?' said Owl, taking it out of Pooh's paw.

'Yes, and I wanted to ask you —'

'Somebody has been keeping honey in it,' said Owl.

'You can keep *anything* in it,' said Pooh earnestly. 'It's Very Useful like that. And I wanted to ask you —'

'You ought to write "A Happy Birthday" on it.'

'*That* was what I wanted to ask you,' said Pooh. 'Because my spelling is Wobbly. It's good spelling but it Wobbles, and the letters get in the wrong places. Would *you* write "A Happy Birthday" on it for me?'

'It's a nice pot,' said Owl, looking at it all round. 'Couldn't I give it too? From both of us?'

'No,' said Pooh. 'That would *not* be a good plan. Now I'll just wash it first, and then you can write on it.'

Well, he washed the pot out, and dried it, while Owl licked the end of his pencil, and wondered how to spell 'birthday'.

'Can you read, Pooh?' he asked a little anxiously. 'There's a notice about knocking and ringing outside my door, which Christopher Robin wrote. Could you read it?'

'Christopher Robin told me what it said, and *then* I could.'

'Well, I'll tell you what *this* says, and then you'll be able to.'

So Owl wrote . . . and this is what he wrote:

HIPY PAPY BTHUTHDTH

THUTHDA BTHUTHDY.

Pooh looked on admiringly.

'I'm just saying "A Happy Birthday",' said Owl carelessly.

'It's a nice long one,' said Pooh, very much impressed by it.

'Well, *actually*, of course, I'm saying "A Very Happy Birthday with love from Pooh." Naturally it takes a good deal of pencil to say a long thing like that.'

'Oh, I see,' said Pooh.

While all this was happening, Piglet had gone back to his own house to get Eeyore's balloon. He held it very tightly against himself, so that it shouldn't blow away, and he ran as fast as he could so as to get to Eeyore before Pooh did; for he thought that he would like to be the first one to give a present, just as if he had thought of it without being told by anybody. And running along, and thinking how pleased Eeyore would be, he didn't look where he was going . . . and suddenly he put his foot in a rabbit hole, and fell down flat on his face.

BANG!!!???***!!!

Piglet lay there, wondering what had happened. At first he thought that the whole world had blown up; and then he thought that perhaps only the Forest part of it had; and then he thought that perhaps only *he* had, and he was now alone in the moon or somewhere, and would never see Christopher Robin or Pooh or Eeyore again. And then he thought, 'Well, even if I'm in the moon, I needn't be face downwards all the time,' so he got cautiously up and looked about him.

He was still in the Forest!

'Well, that's funny,' he thought. 'I wonder what that bang was. I couldn't have made such a noise just falling down. And where's my balloon? And what's that small piece of damp rag doing?'

It was the balloon!

'Oh, dear!' said Piglet. 'Oh, dear, oh, dearie, dearie, dear! Well, it's too late now. I can't go back, and I haven't another balloon, and perhaps Eeyore doesn't *like* balloons so *very* much.'

So he trotted on, rather sadly now, and down he came to the side of the stream where Eeyore was, and called out to him.

'Good morning, Eeyore,' shouted Piglet.

'Good morning, Little Piglet,' said Eeyore. 'If it *is* a good morning,' he said. 'Which I doubt,' said he. 'Not that it matters,' he said.

'Many happy returns of the day,' said Piglet, having now got closer.

Eeyore stopped looking at himself in the stream, and turned to stare at Piglet.

'Just say that again,' he said.

'Many hap —'

'Wait a moment.'

Balancing on three legs, he began to bring his fourth leg very cautiously up to his ear.

'I did this yesterday,' he explained, as he fell down for the third time. 'It's quite easy. It's so as I can hear better. . . . There, that's done it! Now then, what were you saying?' He pushed his ear forward with his hoof.

'Many happy returns of the day,' said Piglet again.

'Meaning me?'

'Of course, Eeyore.'

'My birthday?'

'Yes.'

'Me having a real birthday?'

'Yes, Eeyore, and I've brought you a present.'

Eeyore took down his right hoof from his right ear, turned round, and with great difficulty put up his left hoof.

'I must have that in the other ear,' he said. 'Now then.'

'A present,' said Piglet very loudly.

'Meaning me again?'

'Yes.'

'My birthday still?'

'Of course, Eeyore.'

'Me going on having a real birthday?'

'Yes, Eeyore, and I brought you a balloon.'

'*Balloon?*' said Eeyore. 'You did say balloon? One of those big coloured things you blow up? Gaiety, song-and-dance, here we are and there we are?'

'Yes, but I'm afraid – I'm very sorry, Eeyore – but when I was running along to bring it to you, I fell down.'

'Dear, dear, how unlucky! You ran too fast, I expect. You didn't hurt yourself, Little Piglet?'

'No, but I – I – oh, Eeyore, I burst the balloon!'

There was a very long silence.

'My balloon?' said Eeyore at last.

Piglet nodded.

'My birthday balloon?'

'Yes, Eeyore,' said Piglet, sniffing a little. 'Here it is. With – with many happy returns of the day.' And he gave Eeyore the small piece of damp rag.

'Is this it?' said Eeyore, a little surprised.

Piglet nodded.

'My present?'

Piglet nodded again.

'The balloon?'

'Yes.'

'Thank you, Piglet,' said Eeyore. 'You don't mind my asking,' he went on, 'but what colour was this balloon when it – when it *was* a balloon?'

'Red.'

'I just wondered. . . . Red,' he murmured to himself. 'My favourite colour. . . . How big was it?'

'About as big as me.'

'I just wondered. . . . About as big as Piglet,' he said to himself sadly. 'My favourite size. Well, well.'

Piglet felt very miserable, and didn't know what to say. He was still opening his mouth to begin something, and then deciding that it wasn't any good saying *that*, when he heard a shout from the other side of the river, and there was Pooh.

'Many happy returns of the day,' called out Pooh, forgetting that he had said it already.

'Thank you, Pooh, I'm having them,' said Eeyore gloomily.

'I've brought you a little present,' said Pooh excitedly.

'I've had it,' said Eeyore.

Pooh had now splashed across the stream to Eeyore, and Piglet was sitting a little way off, his head in his paws, snuffling to himself.

'It's a Useful Pot,' said Pooh. 'Here it is. And it's got "A Very Happy Birthday with love from Pooh" written on it. That's what all that writing is. And it's for putting things in. There!'

When Eeyore saw the pot, he became quite excited.

'Why!' he said. 'I believe my Balloon will just go into that Pot!'

'Oh, no, Eeyore,' said Pooh. 'Balloons are much too big to go into Pots. What you do with a balloon is, you hold the balloon —'

'Not mine,' said Eeyore proudly. 'Look, Piglet!' And as Piglet looked sorrowfully round, Eeyore picked the balloon up with his teeth, and placed it carefully in the pot; picked it out and put it on the ground; and then picked it up again and put it carefully back.

'So it does!' said Pooh. 'It goes in!'

'So it does!' said Piglet. 'And it comes out!'

'Doesn't it?' said Eeyore. 'It goes in and out like anything.'

'I'm very glad,' said Pooh happily, 'that I thought of giving you a Useful Pot to put things in.'

'I'm very glad,' said Piglet happily, 'that I thought of giving you Something to put in a Useful Pot.'

But Eeyore wasn't listening. He was taking the balloon out, and putting it back again, as happy as could be. . . .

'And didn't *I* give him anything?' asked Christopher Robin sadly.

'Of course you did,' I said. 'You gave him – don't you remember – a little – a little —'

'I gave him a box of paints to paint things with.'

'That was it.'

'Why didn't I give it to him in the morning?'

'You were so busy getting his party ready for him. He had a cake with icing on the top, and three candles, and his name in pink sugar, and —'

'Yes, *I* remember,' said Christopher Robin.

Us Two

Wherever I am, there's always Pooh,
There's always Pooh and Me.
Whatever I do, he wants to do,
'Where are you going today?' says Pooh:
'Well, that's very odd 'cos I was too.
Let's go together,' says Pooh, says he.
'Let's go together,' says Pooh.

'What's twice eleven?' I said to Pooh,
('Twice what?' said Pooh to Me.)
'I *think* it ought to be twenty-two.'
'Just what I think myself,' said Pooh.
'It wasn't an easy sum to do,
But that's what it is,' said Pooh, said he.
'That's what it is,' said Pooh.

'Let's look for dragons,' I said to Pooh.
'Yes, let's,' said Pooh to Me
We crossed the river and found a few —
'Yes, those are dragons all right,' said Pooh.
'As soon as I saw their beaks I knew.
That's what they are,' said Pooh, said he.
'That's what they are,' said Pooh.

So wherever I am, there's always Pooh,
There's always Pooh and Me.
'What would I do?' I said to Pooh,
'If it wasn't for you,' and Pooh said: 'True,
It isn't much fun for One, but Two
Can stick together,' says Pooh, says he.
'That's how it is,' says Pooh.

Kanga and Baby Roo
Come to the Forest

Nobody seemed to know where they came from, but there they were in the Forest: Kanga and Baby Roo. When Pooh asked Christopher Robin, 'How did they come here?' Christopher Robin said, 'In the Usual Way, if you know what I mean, Pooh,' and Pooh, who didn't, said 'Oh!' Then he nodded his head twice and said, 'In the Usual Way. Ah!'

Then he went to call upon his friend Piglet to see what *he* thought about it. And at Piglet's house he found Rabbit. So they all talked about it together.

'What I don't like about it is this,' said Rabbit. 'Here are we – you, Pooh, and you, Piglet, and Me – and suddenly —'

'And Eeyore,' said Pooh.

'And Eeyore – and then suddenly —'

'And Owl,' said Pooh.

'And Owl – and then all of a sudden —'

'Oh, and Eeyore,' said Pooh. 'I was forgetting *him*.'

'Here – we – are,' said Rabbit very slowly and carefully, 'all – of – us, and then, suddenly, we wake up one morning, and what do we find? We find a Strange Animal among us. An animal of whom we had never even heard before! An animal who carries her family about with her in her pocket! Suppose *I* carried *my* family about with me in *my* pocket, how many pockets should I want?'

'Sixteen,' said Piglet.

'Seventeen, isn't it?' said Rabbit. 'And one more for a handkerchief — that's eighteen. Eighteen pockets in one suit! I haven't time.'

There was a long and thoughtful silence . . . and then Pooh, who had been frowning very hard for some minutes, said: '*I* make it fifteen.'

'What?' said Rabbit.

'Fifteen.'

'Fifteen what?'

'Your family.'

'What about them?'

Pooh rubbed his nose and said that he thought Rabbit had been talking about his family.

'Did I?' said Rabbit carelessly.

'Yes, you said —'

'Never mind, Pooh,' said Piglet impatiently. 'The question is, What are we to do about Kanga?'

'Oh, I see,' said Pooh.

'The best way,' said Rabbit, 'would be this. The best way would be to steal Baby Roo and hide him, and then when Kanga says, "Where's Baby Roo?" we say, "*Aha!*"'

'*Aha!*' said Pooh, practising. '*Aha! Aha!* . . . Of course,' he went on, 'we could say "Aha!" even if we hadn't stolen Baby Roo.'

'Pooh,' said Rabbit kindly, 'you haven't any brain.'

'I know,' said Pooh humbly.

'We say "*Aha!*" so that Kanga knows that *we* know where Baby Roo is. "*Aha!*" means "We'll tell you where Baby Roo is, if you promise to go away from the Forest and never come back." Now don't talk while I think.'

Pooh went into a corner and tried saying 'Aha!' in that sort of voice. Sometimes it seemed to him that it did mean what Rabbit said, and sometimes it seemed to him that it didn't. 'I suppose it's just practice,' he thought. 'I wonder if Kanga will have to practise too so as to understand it.'

'There's just one thing,' said Piglet, fidgeting a bit. 'I was talking to Christopher Robin, and he said that a Kanga was Generally Regarded as One of the Fiercer Animals. I am not frightened of Fierce Animals in the ordinary way, but it is well known that if One of the Fiercer Animals is Deprived of Its Young, it becomes as fierce as Two of the Fiercer Animals. In which case "*Aha!*" is perhaps a *foolish* thing to say.'

'Piglet,' said Rabbit, taking out a pencil, and licking the end of it, 'you haven't any pluck.'

'It is hard to be brave,' said Piglet, sniffing slightly, 'when you're only a Very Small Animal.'

Rabbit, who had begun to write very busily, looked up and said: 'It is because you are a very small animal that you will be Useful in the adventure before us.'

Piglet was so excited at the idea of being Useful that he forgot to be frightened any more, and when Rabbit went on to say that Kangas were only Fierce during the winter months, being at other times of an Affectionate Disposition, he could hardly sit still, he was so eager to begin being useful at once.

'What about me?' said Pooh sadly. 'I suppose *I* shan't be useful?'

'Never mind, Pooh,' said Piglet comfortingly. 'Another time perhaps.'

'Without Pooh,' said Rabbit solemnly as he sharpened his pencil, 'the adventure would be impossible.'

'Oh!' said Piglet, and tried not to look disappointed.

But Pooh went into a corner of the room and said proudly to himself, 'Impossible without Me! *That* sort of Bear.'

'Now listen all of you,' said Rabbit when he had finished writing, and Pooh and Piglet sat listening very eagerly with their mouths open. This was what Rabbit read out:

PLAN TO CAPTURE BABY ROO

1. *General Remarks.* Kanga runs faster than any of Us, even Me.
2. *More General Remarks.* Kanga never takes her eyes off Baby Roo, except when he's safely buttoned up in her pocket.
3. *Therefore.* If we are to capture Baby Roo, we must get a Long Start, because Kanga runs faster than any of Us, even Me. (*See* 1.)
4. *A Thought.* If Roo had jumped out of Kanga's pocket and Piglet had jumped in, Kanga wouldn't know the difference, because Piglet is a Very Small Animal.

5. Like Roo.
6. But Kanga would have to be looking the other way first, so as not to see Piglet jumping in.
7. See 2.
8. *Another Thought*. But if Pooh was talking to her very excitedly, she *might* look the other way for a moment.
9. And then I could run away with Roo.
10. Quickly.
11. *And Kanga wouldn't discover the difference until Afterwards.*

Well, Rabbit read this out proudly, and for a little while after he had read it nobody said anything. And then Piglet, who had been opening and shutting his mouth without making any noise, managed to say very huskily:

'And – Afterwards?'

'How do you mean?'

'When Kanga *does* Discover the Difference?'

'Then we all say "*Aha!*"'

'All three of us?'

'Yes.'

'Oh!'

'Why, what's the trouble, Piglet?'

'Nothing,' said Piglet, 'as long as *we all three* say it. As long as we all three say it,' said Piglet, 'I don't mind,' he said, 'but I shouldn't care to say "*Aha!*" by myself. It wouldn't sound *nearly* so well. By the way,' he said, 'you *are* quite sure about what you said about the winter months?'

'The winter months?'

'Yes, only being Fierce in the Winter Months.'

'Oh, yes, yes, that's all right. Well, Pooh? You see what you have to do?'

'No,' said Pooh Bear. 'Not yet,' he said, 'What *do* I do?'

'Well, you just have to talk very hard to Kanga so as she doesn't notice anything.'

'Oh! What about?'

'Anything you like.'

'You mean like telling her a little bit of poetry or something?'

'That's it,' said Rabbit. 'Splendid. Now come along.'

So they all went out to look for Kanga.

Kanga and Roo were spending a quiet afternoon in a sandy part of the Forest. Baby Roo was practising very small jumps in the sand, and falling down mouse-holes and climbing out of them, and Kanga was fidgeting about and saying 'Just one more jump, dear, and then we must go home.' And at that moment who should come stumping up the hill but Pooh.

'Good afternoon, Kanga.'

'Good afternoon, Pooh.'

'Look at me jumping,' squeaked Roo, and fell into another mouse-hole.

'Hallo, Roo, my little fellow!'

'We were just going home,' said Kanga. 'Good afternoon, Rabbit.

Good afternoon, Piglet.'

Rabbit and Piglet, who had now come up from the other side of the hill, said 'Good afternoon,' and 'Hallo, Roo,' and Roo asked them to look at him jumping, so they stayed and looked.

And Kanga looked too. . . .

'Oh, Kanga,' said Pooh, after Rabbit had winked at him twice, 'I don't know if you are interested in Poetry at all?'

'Hardly at all,' said Kanga.

'Oh!' said Pooh.

'Roo, dear, just one more jump and then we must go home.'

There was a short silence while Roo fell down another mouse-hole.

'Go on,' said Rabbit in a loud whisper behind his paw.

'Talking of Poetry,' said Pooh, 'I made up a little piece as I was coming along. It went like this. Er – now let me see —'

'Fancy!' said Kanga. 'Now Roo, dear —'

'You'll like this piece of poetry,' said Rabbit.

'You'll love it,' said Piglet.

'You must listen very carefully,' said Rabbit.

'So as not to miss any of it,' said Piglet.
'Oh, yes,' said Kanga, but she still looked at Baby Roo.
'*How* did it go, Pooh?' said Rabbit.
Pooh gave a little cough and began.

LINES WRITTEN BY
A BEAR OF VERY LITTLE BRAIN

On Monday, when the sun is hot
I wonder to myself a lot:
'Now is it true, or is it not,
'That what is which and which is what?'

On Tuesday, when it hails and snows,
The feeling on me grows and grows
That hardly anybody knows
If those are these or these are those.

On Wednesday, when the sky is blue,
And I have nothing else to do,
I sometimes wonder if it's true
That who is what and what is who.

On Thursday, when it starts to freeze
And hoar-frost twinkles on the trees,
How very readily one sees
That these are whose — but whose are these?

On Friday —

'Yes, it is, isn't it?' said Kanga, not waiting to hear what happened on Friday. 'Just one more jump, Roo, dear, and then we really *must* be going.'

Rabbit gave Pooh a hurrying-up sort of nudge.

'Talking of Poetry,' said Pooh quickly, 'have you ever noticed that tree right over there?'

'Where?' said Kanga. 'Now, Roo —'

'Right over there,' said Pooh, pointing behind Kanga's back.

'No,' said Kanga. 'Now jump in, Roo, dear, and we'll go home.'

'You ought to look at that tree right over there,' said Rabbit. 'Shall I lift you in, Roo?' And he picked up Roo in his paws.

'I can see a bird in it from here,' said Pooh. 'Or is it a fish?'

'You ought to see that bird from here,' said Rabbit. 'Unless it's a fish.'

'It isn't a fish, it's a bird,' said Piglet.

'So it is,' said Rabbit.

'Is it a starling or a blackbird?' said Pooh.

'That's the whole question,' said Rabbit. 'Is it a blackbird or a starling?'

And then at last Kanga did turn her head to look. And the moment that her head was turned, Rabbit said in a loud voice 'In you go, Roo!' and in jumped Piglet into Kanga's pocket, and off scampered Rabbit, with Roo in his paws, as fast as he could.

'Why, where's Rabbit?' said Kanga, turning round again. 'Are you all right, Roo, dear?'

Piglet made a squeaky Roo-noise from the bottom of Kanga's pocket.

'Rabbit had to go away,' said Pooh. 'I think he thought of something he had to go and see about suddenly.'

'And Piglet?'

'I think Piglet thought of something at the same time. Suddenly.'

'Well, we must be getting home,' said Kanga. 'Good-bye, Pooh.' And in three large jumps she was gone.

Pooh looked after her as she went.

'I wish I could jump like that,' he thought. 'Some can and some can't. That's how it is.'

But there were moments when Piglet wished that Kanga couldn't. Often, when he had had a long walk home through the Forest, he had wished that he were a bird; but now he thought jerkily to himself at the bottom of Kanga's pocket,

'If   is   shall   really   to   take
flying I   never   it.'

And as he went up in the air he said, '*Ooooooo!*' and as he came down he said, '*Ow!*' And he was saying, '*Ooooooo-ow, Ooooooo-ow, Ooooooo-ow*' all the way to Kanga's House.

Of course as soon as Kanga unbuttoned her pocket, she saw what had happened. Just for a moment, she thought she was frightened, and then she knew she wasn't; for she felt sure that Christopher Robin would never let any harm happen to Roo. So she said to herself, 'If they are having a joke with me, I will have a joke with them.'

'Now then, Roo, dear,' she said as she took Piglet out of her pocket. 'Bed-time.'

'*Aha!*' said Piglet, as well as he could after his Terrifying Journey. But it wasn't a very good '*Aha!*' and Kanga didn't seem to understand what it meant.

'Bath first,' said Kanga in a cheerful voice.

'*Aha!*' said Piglet again, looking anxiously for the others. But the others weren't there. Rabbit was playing with Baby Roo in his own house, and feeling more fond of him every minute, and Pooh, who had decided to be a Kanga, was still at the sandy place on the top of the Forest, practising jumps.

'I am not at all sure,' said Kanga in a thoughtful voice, 'that it wouldn't be a good idea to have a *cold* bath this evening. Would you like that, Roo, dear?'

Piglet, who had never been really fond of baths, shuddered a long indignant shudder, and said in as brave a voice as he could: 'Kanga, I see that the time has come to spleak painly.'

'Funny little Roo,' said Kanga, as she got the bath-water ready.

'I am *not* Roo,' said Piglet loudly. 'I am Piglet!'

'Yes, dear, yes,' said Kanga soothingly. 'And imitating Piglet's voice too! So clever of him,' she went on, as she took a large bar of yellow soap out of the cupboard. 'What *will* he be doing next?'

'Can't you *see*?' shouted Piglet. 'Haven't you got *eyes*? *Look* at me!'

'I *am* looking, Roo, dear,' said Kanga rather severely. 'And you know what I told you yesterday about making faces. If you go on making faces like Piglet's you will grow up to *look* like Piglet – and *then* think how sorry you will be. Now then, into the bath, and don't let me have to speak to you about it again.'

Before he knew where he was, Piglet was in the bath, and Kanga was scrubbing him firmly with a large lathery flannel.

'*Ow!*' cried Piglet. 'Let me out! I'm Piglet!'

'Don't open the mouth, dear, or the soap goes in,' said Kanga. 'There! What did I tell you?'

'You – you – you did it on purpose,' spluttered Piglet, as soon as he could speak again . . . and then accidentally had another mouthful of lathery flannel.

'That's right, dear, don't say anything,' said Kanga, and in another minute Piglet was out of the bath, and being rubbed dry with a towel.

'Now,' said Kanga, 'there's your medicine, and then bed.'

'W-w-what medicine?' said Piglet.

'To make you grow big and strong, dear. You don't want to grow up small and weak like Piglet, do you? Well, then!'

At that moment there was a knock at the door.

'Come in,' said Kanga, and in came Christopher Robin.

'Christopher Robin, Christopher Robin!' cried Piglet. 'Tell Kanga who I am! She keeps saying I'm Roo. I'm not Roo, am I!'

Christopher Robin looked at him very carefully, and shook his head.

'You can't be Roo,' he said, 'because I've just seen Roo playing in Rabbit's house.'

'Well!' said Kanga. 'Fancy that! Fancy my making a mistake like that.'

'There you are!' said Piglet. 'I told you so. I'm Piglet.'

Christopher Robin shook his head again.

'Oh, you're not Piglet,' he said. 'I know Piglet well, and he's *quite* a different colour.'

Piglet began to say that this was because he had just had a bath, and then he thought that perhaps he wouldn't say that, and as he opened his mouth to say something else, Kanga slipped the medicine spoon in, and then patted him on the back and told him that it was really quite a nice taste when you got used to it.

'I knew it wasn't Piglet,' said Kanga. 'I wonder who it can be.'

'Perhaps it's some relation of Pooh's,' said Christopher Robin. 'What about a nephew or an uncle or something?'

Kanga agreed that this was probably what it was, and said that they would have to call it by some name.

'I shall call it Pootel,' said Christopher Robin. 'Henry Pootel for short.'

And just when it was decided, Henry Pootel wriggled out of Kanga's arms and jumped to the ground. To his great joy Christopher Robin had left the door open. Never had Henry Pootel Piglet run so fast as he ran then, and he didn't stop running until he had got quite close to his house. But when he was a hundred yards away he stopped running, and rolled the rest of the way home, so as to get his own nice comfortable colour again. . . .

So Kanga and Roo stayed in the Forest. And every Tuesday Roo spent the day with his great friend Rabbit, and every Tuesday Kanga spent the day with her great friend Pooh, teaching him to jump, and every Tuesday Piglet spent the day with his great friend Christopher Robin. So they were all happy again.

The Engineer

Let it rain!
Who cares?
I've a train
Upstairs,
With a brake
Which I make
From a string
Sort of thing,
Which works
In jerks,
'Cos it drops
In the spring,
Which stops
With the string,

And the wheels
All stick
So quick
That it feels
Like a thing
That you make
With a brake,
Not string . . .

So that's what I make,
When the day's all wet.
It's a good sort of brake
But it hasn't worked yet.

Tigger Comes to the Forest and has Breakfast

Winnie-the-Pooh woke up suddenly in the middle of the night and listened. Then he got out of bed, and lit his candle, and stumped across the room to see if anybody was trying to get into his honey-cupboard, and they weren't, so he stumped back again, blew out his candle, and got into bed. Then he heard the noise again.

'Is that you, Piglet?' he said.

But it wasn't.

'Come in, Christopher Robin,' he said.

But Christopher Robin didn't.

'Tell me about it tomorrow, Eeyore,' said Pooh sleepily.

But the noise went on.

'*Worraworraworraworraworra*,' said Whatever-it-was, and Pooh found that he wasn't asleep after all.

'What can it be?' he thought. 'There are lots of noises in the Forest, but this is a different one. It isn't a growl, and it isn't a purr, and it isn't a bark, and it isn't the noise-you-make-before-beginning-a-piece-of-poetry, but it's a noise of some kind, made by a strange animal! And he's making it outside my door. So I shall get up and ask him not to do it.'

He got out of bed and opened his front door.

'Hallo!' said Pooh, in case there was anything outside.

'Hallo!' said Whatever-it-was.

'Oh!' said Pooh. 'Hallo!'

'Hallo!'

'Oh, *there* you are!' said Pooh. 'Hallo!'

'Hallo!' said the Strange Animal, wondering how long this was going on.

Pooh was just going to say 'Hallo!' for the fourth time when he thought that he wouldn't, so he said, 'Who is it?' instead.

'Me,' said a voice.

'Oh!' said Pooh. 'Well, come here.'

So Whatever-it-was came here, and in the light of the candle he and Pooh looked at each other.

'I'm Pooh,' said Pooh.

'I'm Tigger,' said Tigger.

'Oh!' said Pooh, for he had never seen an animal like this before. 'Does Christopher Robin know about you?'

'Of course he does,' said Tigger.

'Well,' said Pooh, 'it's the middle of the night, which is a good time for going to sleep. And tomorrow morning we'll have some honey for breakfast. Do Tiggers like honey?'

'They like everything,' said Tigger cheerfully.

'Then if they like going to sleep on the floor, I'll go back to bed,' said Pooh, 'and we'll do things in the morning. Good Night.' And he got back into bed and went fast asleep.

When he awoke in the morning, the first thing he saw was Tigger, sitting in front of the glass and looking at himself.

'Hallo!' said Pooh.

'Hallo!' said Tigger, 'I've found somebody just like me. I thought I was the only one of them.'

Pooh got out of bed, and began to explain what a looking-glass was, but just as he was getting to the interesting part, Tigger said:

'Excuse me a moment, but there's something climbing up your table,' and with one loud *Worraworraworraworraworra* he jumped at the end of the tablecloth, pulled it to the ground, wrapped himself up in it three times, rolled to the other end of the room, and, after a terrible struggle, got his head into the daylight again, and said cheerfully: 'Have I won?'

'That's my tablecloth,' said Pooh, as he began to unwind Tigger.

'I wondered what it was,' said Tigger.

'It goes on the table and you put things on it.'

'Then why did it try to bite me when I wasn't looking?'

'I don't *think* it did,' said Pooh.

'It tried,' said Tigger, 'but I was too quick for it.'

Pooh put the cloth back on the table, and he put a large honey-pot on the cloth, and they sat down to breakfast. And as soon as they sat down, Tigger took a large mouthful of honey . . . and he looked up at the ceiling with his head on one side, and made exploring noises with his tongue, and considering noises, and what-have-we-got-*here* noises . . . and then he said in a very decided voice:

'Tiggers don't like honey.'

'Oh!' said Pooh, and tried to make it sound Sad and Regretful. 'I thought they liked everything.'

'Everything except honey,' said Tigger.

Pooh felt rather pleased about this, and said that, as soon as he had finished his own breakfast, he would take Tigger round to Piglet's house, and Tigger could try some of Piglet's haycorns.

'Thank you, Pooh,' said Tigger, 'because haycorns is really what Tiggers like best.'

So after breakfast they went round to see Piglet, and Pooh explained as they went that Piglet was a Very Small Animal who didn't like bouncing, and asked Tigger not to be too Bouncy just at first. And Tigger, who had been hiding behind trees and jumping out on Pooh's shadow when it wasn't looking, said that Tiggers were only bouncy before breakfast, and that as soon as they had had a few haycorns they became Quiet and Refined. So by-and-by they knocked at the door of Piglet's house.

'Hallo, Pooh,' said Piglet.

'Hallo, Piglet. This is Tigger.'

'Oh, is it?' said Piglet, and he edged round to the other side of the table. 'I thought Tiggers were smaller than that.'

'Not the big ones,' said Tigger.

'They like haycorns,' said Pooh, 'so that's what we've come for, because poor Tigger hasn't had any breakfast yet.'

Piglet pushed the bowl of haycorns towards Tigger, and said, 'Help yourself,' and then he got close up to Pooh and felt much braver, and said, 'So you're Tigger? Well, well!' in a careless sort of voice. But Tigger said nothing because his mouth was full of haycorns. . . .

After a long munching noise he said:

'Ee-ers o i a-ors.'

And when Pooh and Piglet said 'What?' he said 'Skoos ee,' and went outside for a moment.

When he came back he said firmly:

'Tiggers don't like haycorns.'

'But you said they liked everything except honey,' said Pooh.

'Everything except honey *and* haycorns,' explained Tigger.

When he heard this, Pooh said, 'Oh, I see!' and Piglet, who was rather glad that Tiggers didn't like haycorns, said, 'What about thistles?'

'Thistles,' said Tigger, 'is what Tiggers like best.'

'Then let's go along and see Eeyore,' said Piglet.

So the three of them went; and after they had walked and walked and walked, they came to the part of the Forest where Eeyore was.

'Hallo, Eeyore!' said Pooh. 'This is Tigger.'

'What is?' said Eeyore.

'This,' explained Pooh and Piglet together, and Tigger smiled his happiest smile and said nothing.

Eeyore walked all round Tigger one way, and then turned and walked all round him the other way.

'What did you say it was?' he asked.

'Tigger.'

'Ah!' said Eeyore.

'He's just come,' explained Piglet.

'Ah!' said Eeyore again.

He thought for a long time and then said:

'When is he going?'

86

Pooh explained to Eeyore that Tigger was a great friend of Christopher Robin's, who had come to stay in the Forest, and Piglet explained to Tigger that he mustn't mind what Eeyore said because he was *always* gloomy; and Eeyore explained to Piglet that, on the contrary, he was feeling particularly cheerful this morning; and Tigger explained to anybody who was listening that he hadn't had any breakfast yet.

'I knew there was something,' said Pooh. 'Tiggers always eat thistles, so that was why we came to see you, Eeyore.'

'Don't mention it, Pooh.'

'Oh, Eeyore, I didn't mean that I didn't *want* to see you —'

'Quite – quite. But your new stripy friend – naturally, he wants his breakfast. What did you say his name was?'

'Tigger.'

'Then come this way, Tigger.'

Eeyore led the way to the most thistly-looking patch of thistles that ever was, and waved a hoof at it.

'A little patch I was keeping for my birthday,' he said; 'but, after all, what *are* birthdays? Here today and gone tomorrow. Help yourself, Tigger.'

Tigger thanked him and looked a little anxiously at Pooh.

'Are these really thistles?' he whispered.

'Yes,' said Pooh.

'What Tiggers like best?'

'That's right,' said Pooh.

'I see,' said Tigger.

So he took a large mouthful, and he gave a large crunch.

'*Ow!*' said Tigger.

He sat down and put his paw in his mouth.

'What's the matter?' asked Pooh.

'*Hot!*' mumbled Tigger.

'Your friend,' said Eeyore, 'appears to have bitten on a bee.'

Pooh's friend stopped shaking his head to get the prickles out, and explained that Tiggers didn't like thistles.

'Then why bend a perfectly good one?' asked Eeyore.

'But you said,' began Pooh, '– you *said* that Tiggers liked everything except honey and haycorns.'

'*And* thistles,' said Tigger, who was now running round in circles with his tongue hanging out.

Pooh looked at him sadly.

'What are we going to do?' he asked Piglet.

Piglet knew the answer to that, and he said at once that they must go and see Christopher Robin.

'You'll find him with Kanga,' said Eeyore. He came close to Pooh, and said in a loud whisper:

'*Could* you ask your friend to do his exercises somewhere else? I shall be having lunch directly, and don't want it bounced on just before I begin. A trifling matter, and fussy of me, but we all have our little ways.'

Pooh nodded solemnly and called to Tigger.

'Come along and we'll go and see Kanga. She's sure to have lots of breakfast for you.'

Tigger finished his last circle and came up to Pooh and Piglet.

'Hot!' he explained with a large and friendly smile. 'Come on!' and he rushed off.

Pooh and Piglet walked slowly after him. And as they walked Piglet said nothing because he couldn't think of anything, and Pooh said nothing, because he was thinking of a poem. And when he had thought of it he began:

> What shall we do about poor little Tigger?
> If he never eats nothing he'll never get bigger.
> He doesn't like honey and haycorns and thistles
> Because of the taste and because of the bristles.
> And all the good things which an animal likes
> Have the wrong sort of swallow or too many spikes.

'He's quite big enough anyhow,' said Piglet.

'He isn't *really* very big.'

'Well, he *seems* so.'

Pooh was thoughtful when he heard this, and then he murmured to himself:

> But whatever his weight in pounds,
> shillings, and ounces,
> He always seems bigger because
> of his bounces.

'And that's the whole poem,' he said. 'Do you like it, Piglet?'

'All except the shillings,' said Piglet. 'I don't think they ought to be there.'

'They wanted to come in after the pounds,' explained Pooh, 'so I

let them. It is the best way to write poetry, letting things come.'

'Oh, I didn't know,' said Piglet.

Tigger had been bouncing in front of them all this time, turning round every now and then to ask, 'Is this the way?' – and now at last they came in sight of Kanga's house, and there was Christopher Robin. Tigger rushed up to him.

'Oh, there you are, Tigger!' said Christopher Robin. 'I knew you'd be somewhere.'

'I've been finding things in the Forest,' said Tigger importantly. 'I've found a pooh and a piglet and an eeyore, but I can't find any breakfast.'

Pooh and Piglet came up and hugged Christopher Robin, and explained what had been happening.

'Don't *you* know what Tiggers like?' asked Pooh.

'I expect if I thought very hard I should,' said Christopher Robin, 'but I *thought* Tigger knew.'

'I do,' said Tigger. 'Everything there is in the world except honey and haycorns and – what were those hot things called?'

'Thistles.'

'Yes, and those.'

'Oh, well then, Kanga can give you some breakfast.'

So they went into Kanga's house, and when Roo had said, 'Hallo, Pooh,' and 'Hallo, Piglet' once, and 'Hallo, Tigger' twice, because he had never said it before and it sounded funny, they told Kanga what they wanted, and Kanga said very kindly, 'Well, look in my cupboard,

91

Tigger dear, and see what you'd like.' Because she knew at once that, however big Tigger seemed to be, he wanted as much kindness as Roo.

'Shall I look, too?' said Pooh, who was beginning to feel a little eleven o'clockish. And he found a small tin of condensed milk, and something seemed to tell him that Tiggers didn't like this, so he took it into a corner by itself, and went with it to see that nobody interrupted it.

But the more Tigger put his nose into this and his paw into that, the more things he found which Tiggers didn't like. And when he found everything in the cupboard, and couldn't eat any of it, he said to Kanga, 'What happens now?'

But Kanga and Christopher Robin and Piglet were all standing round Roo, watching him have his Extract of Malt. And Roo was saying, 'Must I?' and Kanga was saying, 'Now, Roo dear, you remember what you promised.'

'What is it?' whispered Tigger to Piglet.

'His Strengthening Medicine,' said Piglet. 'He hates it.'

So Tigger came closer, and he leant over the back of Roo's chair, and suddenly he put out his tongue, and took one large golollop, and, with a sudden jump of surprise, Kanga said, 'Oh!' and then clutched at the spoon again just as it was disappearing, and pulled it safely back out of Tigger's mouth. But the Extract of Malt had gone.

'Tigger *dear!*' said Kanga.

'He's taken my medicine, he's taken my medicine, he's taken my medicine!' sang Roo happily, thinking it was a tremendous joke.

Then Tigger looked up at the ceiling, and closed his eyes, and his tongue went round and round his chops, in case he had left any outside, and a peaceful smile came over his face as he said, 'So *that's* what Tiggers like!'

Which explains why he always lived at Kanga's house afterwards, and had Extract of Malt for breakfast, dinner, and tea. And sometimes, when Kanga thought he wanted strengthening, he had a spoonful or two of Roo's breakfast after meals as medicine.

'But *I* think,' said Piglet to Pooh, 'that he's been strengthened quite enough.'

*I Could Spend
A Happy Morning*

I could spend a happy morning
    Seeing Roo,
I could spend a happy morning
    Being Pooh.
For it doesn't seem to matter,
If I don't get any fatter
(And I *don't* get any fatter),
    What I do.

Oh, I like his way of talking,
    Yes, I do.
It's the nicest way of talking
    Just for two.
And a Help-yourself with Rabbit
Though it may become a habit,
Is a *pleasant* sort of habit
    For a Pooh.

I could spend a happy morning
    Seeing Piglet.
And I couldn't spend a happy morning
    Not seeing Piglet.
And it doesn't seem to matter
If I don't see Owl and Eeyore (or any of the others),
And I'm not going to see Owl or Eeyore
                (or any of the others)
    Or Christopher Robin.

94

The More It Snows

The more it
SNOWS-tiddely-pom,
The more it
GOES-tiddely-pom
The more it
GOES-tiddely-pom
On
Snowing.

And nobody
KNOWS-tiddely-pom,
How cold my
TOES-tiddely-pom
How cold my
TOES-tiddely-pom
Are
Growing.

Hunny

It's very, very funny,
'Cos I *know* I had some honey;
'Cos it had a label on,
    Saying HUNNY.

A goloptious full-up pot too,
And I don't know where it's got to,
No, I don't know where it's gone —
    Well, it's funny.

This Warm and Sunny Spot

This warm and sunny Spot
    Belongs to Pooh.
And here he wonders what
    He's going to do.
Oh, bother, I forgot —
    It's Piglet's too.

Pooh Invents
a New Game

By the time it came to the edge of the Forest the stream had grown up, so that it was almost a river, and, being grown-up, it did not run and jump and sparkle along as it used to do when it was younger, but moved more slowly. For it knew now where it was going, and it said to itself, 'There is no hurry. We shall get there some day.' But all the little streams higher up in the Forest went this way and that, quickly, eagerly, having so much to find out before it was too late.

There was a broad track, almost as broad as a road, leading from the Outland to the Forest, but before it could come to the Forest, it had to cross this river. So, where it crossed, there was a wooden bridge, almost as broad as a road, with wooden rails on each side of it. Christopher Robin could just get his chin on to the top rail, if he wanted to, but it was more fun to stand on the bottom rail, so that he could lean right over, and watch the river slipping slowly away beneath him. Pooh could get his chin on to the bottom rail if he wanted to, but it was more fun to lie down and get his head under it, and watch the river slipping slowly away beneath him. And this was the only way in which Piglet and Roo could watch the river at all, because they were too small to reach the bottom rail. So they would lie down and watch it . . . and it slipped away very slowly, being in no hurry to get there.

One day, when Pooh was walking towards this bridge, he was trying to make up a piece of poetry about fir-cones, because there they were, lying about on each side of him, and he felt singy. So he picked a fir-cone up, and looked at it, and said to himself, 'This is a very good fir-cone, and something ought to rhyme to it.' But he couldn't think of anything. And then this came into his head suddenly:

> Here is a myst'ry
> About a little fir-tree.
> Owl says it's *his* tree,
> And Kanga says it's *her* tree.

'Which doesn't make sense,' said Pooh, 'because Kanga doesn't live in a tree.'

He had just come to the bridge; and not looking where he was going, he tripped over something, and the fir-cone jerked out of his paw into the river.

'Bother,' said Pooh, as it floated slowly under the bridge, and he went back to get another fir-cone which had a rhyme to it. But then he thought that he would just look at the river instead, because it was a peaceful sort of day, so he lay down and looked at it, and it slipped slowly away beneath him . . . and suddenly, there was his fir-cone slipping away too.

'That's funny,' said Pooh. 'I dropped it on the other side,' said Pooh, 'and it came out on this side! I wonder if it would do it again?' And he went back for some more fir-cones.

It did. It kept on doing it. Then he dropped two in at once, and leant over the bridge to see which of them would come out first; and one of them did; but as they were both the same size, he didn't know if it was the one which he wanted to win, or the other one. So the next time he dropped one big one and one little one, and the big one came out first, which was what he had said it would do, and the little one came out last, which was what he had said it would do, so he had won twice . . . and when he went home for tea, he had won thirty-six and lost twenty-eight, which meant that he was – that he had – well, you take twenty-eight from thirty-six, and *that's* what he was. Instead of the other way round.

And that was the beginning of the game called Poohsticks, which Pooh invented, and which he and his friends used to play on the edge of the Forest. But they played with sticks instead of fir-cones, because they were easier to mark.

Now one day Pooh and Piglet and Rabbit and Roo were all playing Poohsticks together. They had dropped their sticks in when Rabbit said 'Go!' and then they had hurried across to the other side of the bridge, and now they were all leaning over the edge, waiting to see whose stick would come out first. But it was a long time coming, because the river was very lazy that day, and hardly seemed to mind if it didn't ever get there at all.

'I can see mine!' cried Roo. 'No, I can't it's something else. Can you see yours, Piglet? I thought I could see mine, but I couldn't. There it is! No, it isn't. Can you see yours, Pooh?'

'No,' said Pooh.

'I expect my stick's stuck,' said Roo. 'Rabbit, my stick's stuck. Is your stick stuck, Piglet?'

'They always take longer than you think,' said Rabbit.

'How long do you *think* they'll take?' asked Roo.

'I can see yours, Piglet,' said Pooh suddenly.

'Mine's a sort of greyish one,' said Piglet, not daring to lean too far over in case he fell in.

'Yes, that's what I can see. It's coming over on to my side.'

Rabbit leant over further than ever, looking for his, and Roo wriggled up and down, calling out 'Come on, stick! Stick, stick, stick!' and Piglet got very excited because his was the only one which had been seen, and that meant that he was winning.

'It's coming!' said Pooh.

'Are you *sure* it's mine?' squeaked Piglet excitedly.

'Yes, because it's grey. A big grey one. Here it comes! A very – big – grey – Oh, no, it isn't, it's Eeyore.'

And out floated Eeyore.

'Eeyore!' cried everybody.

Looking very calm, very dignified, with his legs in the air, came Eeyore from beneath the bridge.

'It's Eeyore!' cried Roo, terribly excited.

'Is that so?' said Eeyore, getting caught up by a little eddy, and turning slowly round three times. 'I wondered.'

'I didn't know you were playing,' said Roo.

'I'm not,' said Eeyore.

'Eeyore, what *are* you doing there?' said Rabbit.

'I'll give you three guesses, Rabbit. Digging holes in the ground? Wrong. Leaping from branch to branch of a young oak-tree? Wrong. Waiting for somebody to help me out of the river? Right. Give Rabbit time, and he'll always get the answer.'

'But, Eeyore,' said Pooh in distress, 'what can we – I mean, how shall we – do you think if we —'

'Yes,' said Eeyore. 'One of those would be just the thing. Thank you, Pooh.'

'He's going *round* and *round*,' said Roo, much impressed.

'And why not?' said Eeyore coldly.

'I can swim too,' said Roo proudly.

'Not round and round,' said Eeyore. 'It's much more difficult. I didn't want to come swimming at all to-day,' he went on, revolving slowly. 'But if, when in, I decide to practise a slight circular movement from right to left – or perhaps I should say,' he added, as he got into another eddy, 'from left to right, just as it happens to occur to me, it is nobody's business but my own.'

There was a moment's silence while everybody thought.

'I've got a sort of idea,' said Pooh at last, 'but I don't suppose it's a very good one.'

'I don't suppose it is either,' said Eeyore.

'Go on, Pooh,' said Rabbit. 'Let's have it.'

'Well, if we all threw stones and things into the river on *one* side of Eeyore, the stones would make waves, and the waves would wash him to the other side.'

'That's a very good idea,' said Rabbit, and Pooh looked happy again.

'Very,' said Eeyore. 'When I want to be washed, Pooh, I'll let you know.'

'Supposing we hit him by mistake?' said Piglet anxiously.

'Or supposing you missed him by mistake,' said Eeyore. 'Think of all the possibilities, Piglet, before you settle down to enjoy yourselves.'

But Pooh had got the biggest stone he could carry, and was leaning over the bridge, holding it in his paws.

'I'm not throwing it, I'm dropping it, Eeyore,' he explained. 'And then I can't miss – I mean I can't hit you. *Could* you stop turning round for a moment, because it muddles me rather?'

'No,' said Eeyore. 'I *like* turning round.'

Rabbit began to feel that it was time he took command.

'Now, Pooh,' he said, 'when I say "Now!" you can drop it. Eeyore, when I say "Now!" Pooh will drop his stone.'

'Thank you very much, Rabbit, but I expect I shall know.'

'Are you ready, Pooh? Piglet, give Pooh a little more room. Get back a bit there, Roo. Are you ready?'

'No,' said Eeyore.

'*Now!*' said Rabbit.

Pooh dropped his stone. There was a loud splash, and Eeyore disappeared . . .

It was an anxious moment for the watchers on the bridge. They looked and looked . . . and even the sight of Piglet's stick coming out a little in front of Rabbit's didn't cheer them up as much as you would have expected. And then, just as Pooh was beginning to think that he must have chosen the wrong stone or the wrong river or the wrong day for his Idea, something grey showed for a moment by the river bank . . . and it got slowly bigger and bigger . . . and at last it was Eeyore coming out.

With a shout they rushed off the bridge, and pushed and pulled at him; and soon he was standing among them again on dry land.

'Oh, Eeyore, you *are* wet!' said Piglet, feeling him.

Eeyore shook himself, and asked somebody to explain to Piglet what happened when you had been inside a river for quite a long time.

'Well done, Pooh,' said Rabbit kindly. 'That was a good idea of ours.'

'What was?' asked Eeyore.

'Hooshing you to the bank like that.'

'*Hooshing* me?' said Eeyore in surprise. 'Hooshing *me*? You didn't think I was *hooshed*, did you? I dived. Pooh dropped a large stone on me, and so as not to be struck heavily on the chest, I dived and swam to the bank.'

'You didn't really,' whispered Piglet to Pooh, so as to comfort him.

'I didn't *think* I did,' said Pooh anxiously.

'It's just Eeyore,' said Piglet. '*I* thought your Idea was a very good Idea.'

Pooh began to feel a little more comfortable, because when you are a Bear of Very Little Brain, and you Think of Things, you find sometimes that a Thing which seemed very Thingish inside you is quite different when it gets out into the open and has other people looking at it. And, anyhow, Eeyore *was* in the river, and now he *wasn't*, so he hadn't done any harm.

'How did you fall in, Eeyore?' asked Rabbit, as he dried him with Piglet's handkerchief.

'I didn't,' said Eeyore.

'But how —'

'I was BOUNCED,' said Eeyore.

'Oo,' said Roo excitedly, 'did somebody push you?'

'Somebody BOUNCED me. I was just thinking by the side of the river –

thinking, if any of you know what that means – when I received a loud BOUNCE.'

'Oh, Eeyore!' said everybody.

'Are you sure you didn't slip?' asked Rabbit wisely.

'Of course I slipped. If you're standing on the slippery bank of a river, and somebody BOUNCES you loudly from behind, you slip. What did you think I did?'

'But who did it?' asked Roo.

Eeyore didn't answer.

'I expect it was Tigger,' said Piglet nervously.

'But, Eeyore,' said Pooh, 'was it a Joke, or an Accident? I mean —'

'I didn't stop to ask, Pooh. Even at the very bottom of the river I didn't stop to say to myself, "*Is* this a Hearty Joke, or is it the Merest Accident?" I just floated to the surface, and said to myself, "It's wet." If you know what I mean.'

'And where was Tigger?' asked Rabbit.

Before Eeyore could answer, there was a loud noise behind them, and through the hedge came Tigger himself.

'Hallo, everybody,' said Tigger cheerfully.

'Hallo, Tigger,' said Roo.

Rabbit became very important suddenly.

'Tigger,' he said solemnly, 'what happened just now?'

'Just when?' said Tigger a little uncomfortably.

'When you bounced Eeyore into the river.'

'I didn't bounce him.'

'You bounced me,' said Eeyore gruffly.

'I didn't really. I had a cough, and I happened to be behind Eeyore, and I said "*Grrrr – oppp – ptschschschz*".'

'Why?' said Rabbit, helping Piglet up, and dusting him. 'It's all right, Piglet.'

'It took me by surprise,' said Piglet nervously.

'That's what I call bouncing,' said Eeyore. 'Taking people by surprise. Very unpleasant habit. I don't mind Tigger being in the Forest,' he went on, 'because it's a large Forest, and there's plenty of room to bounce in it. But I don't see why he should come into *my* little corner of it, and bounce there. It isn't as if there was anything very wonderful about my little corner. Of course for people who like cold, wet, ugly bits it *is* something rather special, but otherwise it's just a corner, and if anybody feels bouncy —'

'I didn't bounce, I coughed,' said Tigger crossly.

'Bouncy or coffy, it's all the same at the bottom of the river.'

'Well,' said Rabbit, 'all I can say is – well, here's Christopher Robin, so *he* can say it.'

Christopher Robin came down from the Forest to the bridge, feeling all sunny and careless, and just as if twice nineteen didn't matter a bit, as it didn't on such a happy afternoon, and he thought that if he stood on the bottom rail of the bridge, and leant over, and watched the river slipping slowly away beneath him, then he would suddenly know everything that there was to be known, and he would be able to tell Pooh, who wasn't quite sure about some of it. But when he got to the bridge and saw all the animals there, then he knew that it wasn't that kind of afternoon, but the other kind, when you wanted to *do* something.

'It's like this, Christopher Robin,' began Rabbit. 'Tigger —'

'No, I didn't,' said Tigger.

'Well, anyhow, there I was,' said Eeyore.

'But I don't think he meant to,' said Pooh.

'He just *is* bouncy,' said Piglet, 'and he can't help it.'

'Try bouncing *me*, Tigger,' said Roo eagerly. 'Eeyore, Tigger's going to try *me*. Piglet, do you think —'

'Yes, yes,' said Rabbit, 'we don't all want to speak at once. The point is, what does Christopher Robin think about it?'

'All I did was I coughed,' said Tigger.

'He bounced,' said Eeyore.

'Well, I sort of boffed,' said Tigger.

'Hush!' said Rabbit, holding up his paw. 'What does Christopher Robin think about it all? That's the point.'

'Well,' said Christopher Robin, not quite sure what it was all about. '*I* think —'

'Yes?' said everybody.

'*I* think we all ought to play Poohsticks.'

So they did. And Eeyore, who had never played it before, won more times than anybody else; and Roo fell in twice, the first time by accident and the second time on purpose, because he suddenly saw Kanga coming from the Forest, and he knew he'd have to go to bed anyhow. So then Rabbit said he'd go with them; and Tigger and Eeyore went off together, because Eeyore wanted to tell Tigger How to Win at Poohsticks, which you do by letting your stick drop in a twitchy sort of way, if you understand what I mean, Tigger; and Christopher Robin and Pooh and Piglet were left on the bridge by themselves.

For a long time they looked at the river beneath them, saying nothing, and the river said nothing too, for it felt very quiet and peaceful on this summer afternoon.

'Tigger is all right, *really*,' said Piglet lazily.

'Of course he is,' said Christopher Robin.

'Everybody is *really*,' said Pooh. 'That's what *I* think,' said Pooh. 'But I don't suppose I'm right,' he said.

'Of course you are,' said Christopher Robin.

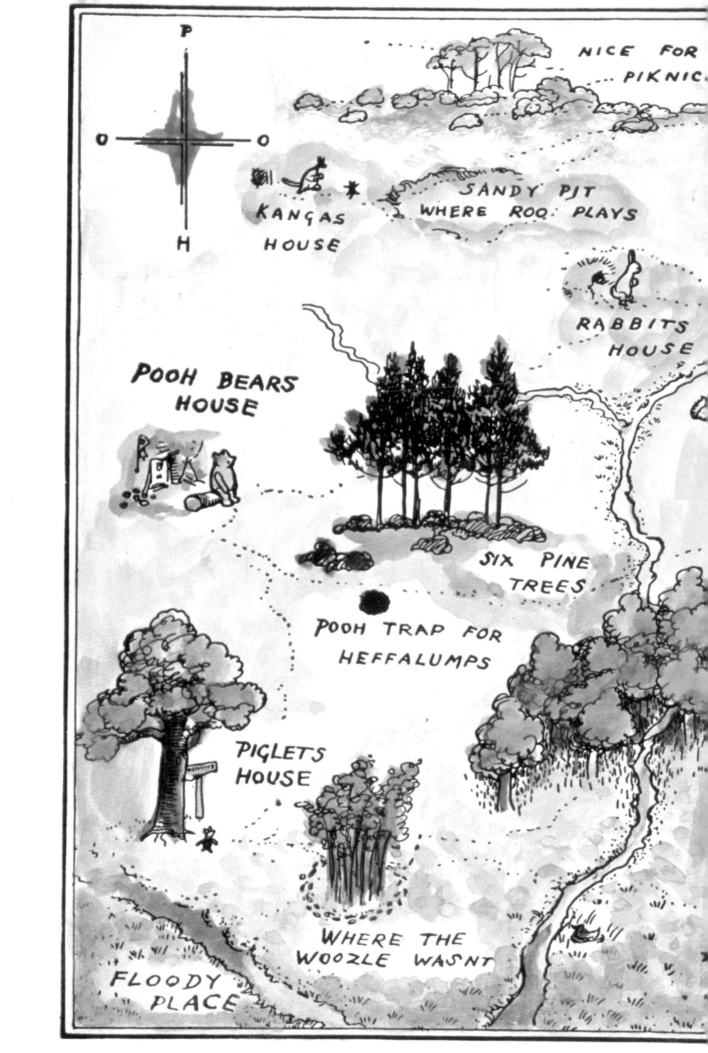